This book belongs to

_____

Hello, Geneseo

Colleen N. Venturino

Illustrated by Lea Embeli

ORONOKA PRESS

ISBN 978-1-7338387-0-2 (paperback)

First paperback edition 2019

Published by Oronoka Press

Inquiries: oronokapress@gmail.com

For my grandson, Luke. Love you forever.
Inspired by Claire, Mark, Christian, and young-at-heart Mike

Hello! Come along with me and we can explore Geneseo.

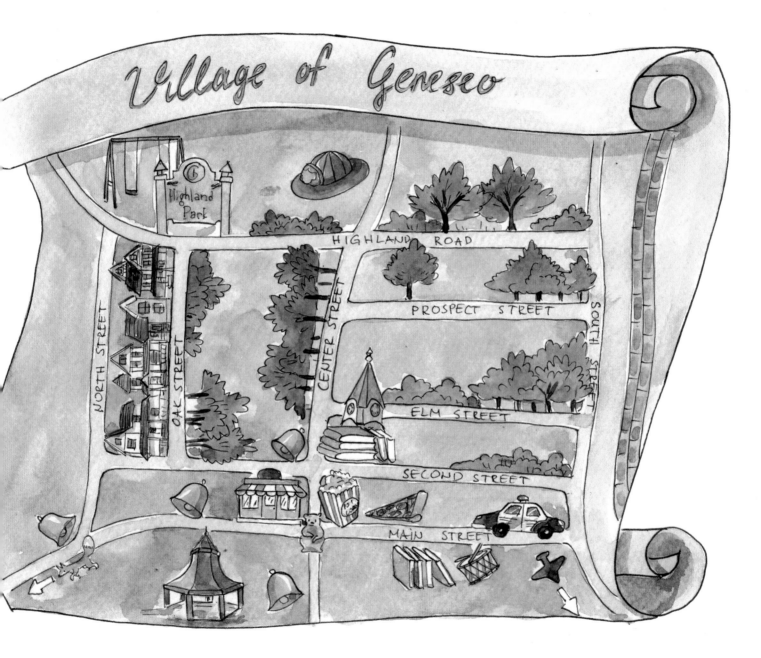

As you read this book, can you find the places on this map?

See the big old houses on
Oak Street.

What a fun
neighborhood!

Highland Park has the best playground ever.
The sliding board and swing set are my favorite things in the park.

In the winter we can
skate and play hockey.

What do you like best
at Highland Park?

Have you heard the bells on Center Street ring every hour? You can count the bells ringing to tell what time it is.

Geneseo has many bell towers.

My mom takes me to storytime at the library.

We walk to the movie theater for a movie and popcorn.

Pizza for lunch on Main Street with mom and dad is a great treat.

We see the friendly officer on Main Street.
He keeps us safe in the Village.

I like to visit my favorite stores on Main Street.

Hello, Bronze Bear. You are in the middle of Main Street.
Be careful of the cars and trucks!

Look at all the books and toys
in the shop window.

Brave Geneseo firefighters are the "Protectors of the Valley." Look for these words on the door of the Geneseo fire truck.

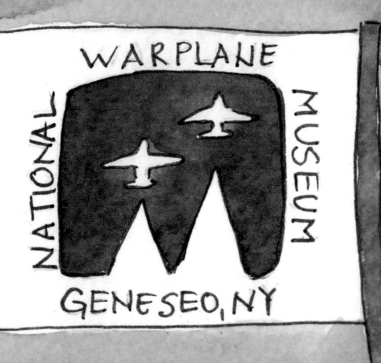

NATIONAL WARPLANE MUSEUM GENESEO, NY

We visit the
airplane museum
down in the valley.

Someday I would like to fly a plane over Geneseo.

Can you see the old oak trees?

Horses, riders, and hounds,
what are you looking for?

Look at the beautiful sunset. It's been a long day. Good night, Geneseo.

Made in the USA
Monee, IL
19 December 2020